Achoo!

by Mij Kelly and

Mary McQuillan

First edition for the United States, its territories and dependencies, and Canada published in 2009 by Barron's Educational Series, Inc.

First published in 2007 by Hodder Children's Books

All inquiries should be addressed to:
Barron's Educational Series, Inc.
250 Wireless Boulevard
Hauppauge, New York 11788
www.barronseduc.com

ISBN-13: 978-0-7641-6969-4
ISBN-10: 0-7641-6969-6

Library of Congress Control Number: 2008944226

Printed in China

9 8 7 6 5 4 3 2 1

AchoO!

MIJ KELLY   MARY McQUILLAN

BARRON'S

This is the story of Suzy Sue,
and the fateful day
when she went...

Her friends who knew all
the social graces, and didn't
like germs being spat in their
faces cried,

"Suzy Sue!
Please!
Please!
Please!
Cover your mouth
if you're going
to sneeze!"

"I'm ever-so-sorry,"
said Suzy Sue.
"I just didn't know
that's what I should do."

Well, that raised a rumpus…

"She hasn't a clue!"

"The child's got no manners!"

"Was she born in a ZOO?"

"It's true," said the cow. "She is **horribly** rude, but that **doesn't** mean she can't be improved.

If we teach her the **rules,** I'm sure we can save her from a life of bad manners and ghastly behavior."

Good Manners Can Be Contagious!

Rule Number 1 is don't be disgusting.

"Well look whose **manners** need some adjusting!"

"This dog is not doing anything **right.** He's **grotty,** he's **snotty,** his **stench** causes **fright!**"

"Take a **bath** and **brush** your teeth.
Learn to use a **handkerchief**.
If you've got a **runny** nose,
please don't wipe it
on your clothes!"

Rule Number 2 is don't eat like a pig.

"Look at them slurping. They don't care a bit.
Surely they know it's **revolting** and **rude**
to wallow about like that in
your food."

"Wash your hands before you eat.
Don't stand in your dinner. Sit in your seat.
Try not to burp and whatever you do,
keep your mouth shut when you chew!"

Rule Number 3 is do not fight.

"Some people can't tell what's
wrong from what's right.

Just look at these cats!

They lack poise.

They lack charm.

They're a social disaster,
a disgrace to the farm!"

"Say please and thank you.
Always play fair.
And whatever you do,

SHARE!
SHARE!
SHARE!"

"That's it," said the cow.
"Those are the **rules**.
Three **pearls** of wisdom –
absolute **jewels**."

"Don't stink like a dog,

or

eat like a pig!

Don't fight like a cat,

it's not clever or big!"

The cats and pigs were up in arms.
So were their friends from other farms.

"They spoiled our game of tug-of-war!"

"We don't like them anymore!"

"They ruined our meal!"

"They made us cry!"

"I don't really smell... do I?"

"Look what you've done," said Suzy Sue.
"Your friends are **really** mad at you.
You hurt their feelings. You were cruel.
You broke the most important rule."

The *golden rule* is always do
what you'd like others to do to you.

"That means **be kind**," said Suzy Sue.
"Remember, they've got feelings, too."

"When you told me
I smelled bad,
you made me
feel really sad."

"Oh darn!" said the sheep.
"We can't tell the dog
he's a horrible, stinky,
filthy old slob."

"But maybe we can
give him hints –
like a bubble bath,
or peppermints."

Good
Manners
Can Be
Contagious!

"If you're kind," said Suzy Sue,
"people sometimes learn from you."

"You pushed me around.
Can't you see?
You can't teach me
manners by bullying me."

Cows are rude!

"Botheration!"
said
the
horse.

"We can't
make pigs
change by using force.
But if we make sure
that we're polite,
they'll copy us and get it right."

Good
Manners
Can Be
Contagious!

"If you're kind," said Suzy Sue,
"people will be kind to you."

"You chopped our tug-of-war
in two. We never want
to speak to you."

"Oh dear," said the goat,
"we made a mistake – though
with cats such mistakes
are easy to make!

But if we're
sorry and
make amends,
maybe...

...we can all be friends!"

After that, things were
sweet and light.
They all helped each
other to be polite.

The pigs sipped from tea cups.
The dog took a shower.
The cats skipped around,
handing out flowers.

And when they gave one to Suzy Sue,

A A A . . .

"Would you like a hanky?"

"Yes, thank you."

"You'd **never** believe she was born in a zoo!"

Suzy Sue – 6 months